FEB 24 1997

HOWARD AND THE SITTER SURPRISE

Priscilla Paton • *Illustrated by Paul Meisel*

Houghton Mifflin Company Boston 1996

For information about this and other Houghton Mifflin
trade and reference books and multimedia products,
visit The Bookstore at Houghton Mifflin on the
World Wide Web at http://www.hmco.com/trade/.

Manufactured in the United States of America

Book Design by David Saylor
The text of this book is set in 15-point Zapf International Medium.
The illustrations are watercolor and ink, reproduced in full color.

HOR 10 9 8 7 6 5 4 3 2 1

Library of Congress Cataloging-in-Publication Data
Paton, Priscilla.
Howard and the babysitter surprise / Priscilla Paton ;
illustrated by Paul Meisel.   p.   cm.
Summary: A little boy refuses to behave for his
babysitters until Sarah the bear wins him over.
ISBN 0-395-71814-7
[1. Babysitters—Fiction. 2. Behavior—Fiction.
3. Bears—Fiction.] I. Meisel, Paul. II. Title.
PZ7.P27344Ho 1996
[Fic]—dc20 94-38422   CIP   AC

For my parents and for my cubs,
James and Elizabeth
—P. M. P.

For Grammy Cammy,
and Charles
—P. M.

Howard hated baby sitters. When a sitter came, he'd block the door!

Norman and Jill
would yell for Mom.
Mom would kiss
Howard and hand him
to the sitter. But as soon
as she was gone,
Howard would break
away. He'd climb,
he'd throw, he'd howl!

After an evening with
Howard, sitters never returned.

When Jane came, Howard climbed on the porch roof and threw sock bombs. When Bill came, Howard climbed on top of the refrigerator and tossed marshmallows.

When Roland came,
he taught Howard how to
juggle—and Howard liked
him! Then Howard juggled
with pickles and eggs.
Somehow, Roland never
came back.

Jenny and Ralph kept Howard off the roof. They kept him away from pickles and eggs. But nobody could keep Howard in bed! Norman and Jill would wake up late at night and peek into the living room. Howard and the sitter would be eating pizza and watching TV.

Howard always got away with it!

One summer night Mom said, "I've found
a new sitter. Her name is Sarah. She lives
in the forest behind our house. She'll come
when I blow this whistle."

Howard stared at her. "That's crazy! Use
the phone, Mom." But Mom blew the whistle . . .

. . . and Sarah came to the door. Howard's hair stood on end!

"Come now," said Mom. "Say hello to Sarah." Sarah smiled sweetly. Her teeth were as long as Howard's fingers! She gave Howard a big hug. His eyes bugged out! Then she picked up Norman and Jill with her long claws. Sarah was strong!

"They're as cute as my own," Sarah said to Mom. "They'll be safe with me."

BETA E. KING LIBRARY

Safe?! The children wondered.
Would they be the snack tonight?
And would Howard act out?

Howard tried to run away—
but he had only two legs
and Sarah ran on four.

He climbed the refrigerator—
Sarah pulled him down.

He hollered—
Sarah roared louder.

So finally Howard tried to grin her down—
but look at *her* toothy grin!

Howard was mad. His face turned red.
He held his breath until his face turned blue.
Norman and Jill called for Sarah: "Howard's
blue again, Howard's blue!"

Sarah grabbed Howard
in her huge claws and
tossed him in the air.
She tossed him up and down
until he giggled and giggled
and his face turned red again.
Sarah sat him down.

"Howard," she said, "you
must behave!" Howard
looked at his toes. Sarah
waited. He looked at Sarah.

She surprised him! Sarah picked Howard
up with a hug and said to Norman and Jill,
"Storytime!" They made a den under the
table and Sarah told a story. It was about a
cub named Howard.

Howard the cub got mad when his mother left him with a moose. He ran up a tree and threw pine cones.

Then Howard grew
tired and hungry, but he
couldn't get down. And
the poor moose couldn't
help him. They waited
a long, long time for
Howard's mother, who
was not happy to see
her cub up the tree.

"Do you know what?" Sarah said to the children.
"Howard the cub thought his mother didn't love
him when she left him with the nice moose. But
she loved him very much. Sometimes big bears
need to do big bear business, and have big bear fun."

"I know that!" said Howard,
and Norman and Jill nodded too.

The children leaned against Sarah—
she was soft and warm!

"We want another story!" they said.
So Sarah told them the story about a girl
named Goldilocks.

"It's a sad, sad story," Sarah sighed.
"Think of the little baby bear with no
porridge, no chair, and a messy bed!"

"Goldilocks should take a new chair
to Baby Bear," Jill said.

"I'd shut Goldilocks in the closet!"
Howard piped up.

Norman was asleep. So Sarah tucked
them all into bed.

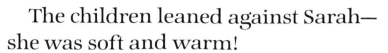

But Jill and Norman woke up later.
They heard a noise! They crawled
out of their rooms, like little cubs.
They peeked into the living room.
Howard was sitting on Sarah's comfy
lap, eating popcorn, and looking at
a book with her.

Howard always got away with it!